TOKOYO

THE SAMURAI'S DAUGHTER

WRITTEN BY

FAITH L. JUSTICE

ILLUSTRATED BY

KAYLA GILLIAM

Tokoyo, The Samurai's Daughter

ACKNOWLEDGEMENTS

It's rare that an author writes a book all by herself and I'm no exception. Thanks to Nathan Reynolds, teacher at Leipsic Elementary School, Ohio, for helping me find great fifth grade beta readers. My very special thanks to Elyssabeth, Jeremy, Juan, Seth, and Sofeea for reading an early draft of this story and giving me feedback. A few adults also took an early peek. Thanks to librarian Redona Klinkenborg, and teacher Hope Justice, at Creekview Ranch School, California.

Kayla Gilliam contributed much more than just beautiful illustrations. She did additional research, corrected some of my Japanese words, and wrote the Cultural Note. Thanks to all of you for your unique insights and helping to make this the best possible book.

CONTENTS

LIST OF ILLUSTRATIONS

X

1

TOKOYO AND THE AMA

AD 1319, the third year of Hojo Takatoki's regency for

Shogun Prince Morikuni

I PUT THE LAST OYSTER in the net bag attached to my belt and clasped my knife between my teeth. I looked up through the clear water to the shimmering spot that was the sun. The other divers—the Ama—were already near the top. My lungs began to burn—a sure sign I needed to return to the surface.

I scanned the rocks and corals for sharks. I had fought off a reef shark once and didn't want to do it again.

All clear.

I pushed off from the sandy bottom, kicking and stroking my way to the surface.

Halfway there, the need for air became almost unbearable. My heart beat faster and I wanted to gasp for air. My strokes became more desperate.

I shouldn't have stayed down so long.

I pushed the panic away. My eyes unfocussed and I entered a calm place. My father's voice echoed softly in my mind leading me through the meditation exercises that all samurai practiced.

My heart slowed. My lungs no longer labored. My strokes pulled me through the last feet of water.

As I broke the surface, I released the air in my lungs slowly with a whistling sound—one of the tricks the Ama use to hold their breath for the deep dives.

"Tokoyo, you worried us!" Hana, my best friend among the Ama, scolded. "I was about to dive back down and drag you up by the hair."

"No need." I took a deep breath of the salty sea air and smiled at my friend.

"Don't take such risks, samurai's daughter." Namika, the oldest diver at sixty-three years, scowled at me. "You have much to learn."

"I'm sorry, Namika." My stomach tightened at the rebuke. I tried hard to be a good Ama, but never seemed to live up to Namika's standards. "I won't stay down so long again."

"Time to get back. We've been out for three hours this afternoon." The old woman headed back to the shore with fast efficient strokes.

"Forgive her sharp tongue." Hana shaded her eyes as she watched Namika swim away. "She grieves for her daughter who dove too deep and stayed down too long. Her son-in-law blames Namika for his wife's death. He keeps his daughters from her, afraid they will want to be Ama like their mother and grandmother."

"I didn't know!" What a horrible fate for the old woman, cut off from her family. I had only my father and missed him terribly when he left to give service to his lord. If he died in battle, I'd have no reason to live.

A wave slapped my face with cold water and I spluttered.

"Hungry?" Hana grinned

"Yes!" My stomach rumbled in reply.

"Last one in has to clean the cuttlefish!" Hana cried and took off for the shore. The other Ama stroked toward the rocky beach.

"No fair!" I shouted. They had a three-stroke lead.

2

THE PEARL

I SWAM MY BEST, but the Ama were born to this life and swam like dolphins. I had other duties as the daughter of a noble samurai and dove only a day or two a week for the pleasure of it. I staggered onto the beach last, to the friendly hoots of the women and girls.

"Come, Tokoyo." Hana gave me a hand. "Let's get you by the fire. Your teeth are chattering so loud they scare the seagulls!"

We gathered around a driftwood fire. I rubbed the goosebumps that rose on my arms trying to drive the chill from my flesh. The other women smiled and joked as we pulled on warm clothes. In the cold sea we wore only a *fundoshi*—a loincloth—and a bandana marked with protective blessings called a *tenugui* to hold our hair.

"Girls!" Namika clapped her hands. A couple of the women who had children rolled their eyes at each other, but didn't complain. Namika was the age of their mothers and their undisputed leader. "Back to the *amagoya*. Let's see what Goddess Funadama provided us today."

We grabbed our bags and trudged up the beach to the Ama house. The *amagoya* sat on a rocky ridge, perched above the sea, sheltered by several twisted pine trees. The other Ama stayed there during the diving season, but I went home to my father's estate on the outer edge of the village at the end of the day.

We trooped onto the wooden porch to sort our take. Funadama, the goddess of the sea, gave us a good catch: several dozen prized abalone and oysters, a couple small squid, and a heap of seaweed. All would bring a good price in the local market.

I pried open my last oyster and gasped.

"Look!" I turned to Hana and showed her a pearl the size of the tip of my little finger. "A pearl of great worth!"

Hana's eyes grew big. "Funadama blessed you, my friend. That's the biggest pearl I've seen. You'll have the merchants fighting for that one."

I looked at the faces surrounding me, most

beamed with pleasure, a couple showed traces of envy. I realized the difference this pearl would make in their lives, whereas I had everything I needed and more. But how to give it to them without offending their pride?

"Namika." I kneeled at the old Ama's feet holding out the shining pearl. "You are older and wiser than all of us. You know best how to bargain with the merchants. Please take this pearl as payment for all you have taught me and share it among the Ama."

"Look at me, child."

I raised my eyes to her wise ones. She understood my plan.

"This is a great gift." She touched the pearl on my palm.

"No greater than the gift you have given me: strength, skill, acceptance, love. Please take it as a sign of the great respect in which I hold you and all Ama."

She took the pearl and the other Ama cheered.

"For that, you don't have to clean the cuttlefish." Hana laughed "Today!"

I glowed with pleasure. I had helped my friends; made their lives easier. We went into the house and relaxed by the fire, eating a meal of rice, seaweed, and fish.

3

AN ADVENTUROUS GIRL

WHEN I SAW NAMIKA leave the house, I poured another bowl of tea and followed.

She sat on a driftwood log, eyes closed, face raised to the lowering sun. She seemed so sad, I decided to leave and turned to go back in.

"Join me, Tokoyo." She patted the log beside her, eyes still closed.

I sat. "How did you know it was me?"

"The wooden porch. Every footfall sounds different." She turned her face to me and opened her eyes. "Most sound like farmers tromping through fields. You, child, have the light step of a dancer."

I held out the bowl. "I brought you more tea."

"Thank you." She sniffed the steam and took a sip. "Just as I like it—hot and bitter."

She set the bowl aside and stretched her arms overhead. I heard small cracking sounds as she moved her head from side to side. She looked at me, head tilted on her shoulder like a bird. "You stayed down for longer than you should today–longer than I did and I'm the best."

"I'm sorry to have worried you." I hung my head.

"You don't understand, child." She cupped my face in her hands. "You showed great skill. Many girls your age would panic and drown when their lungs burn for air. That's why we start the youngsters close to shore gathering seaweed in the shallower water. They learn the advanced skills later. My own daughter..." tears filled her eyes. She turned from me. "What did you do? How did you survive?"

"My father taught me to calm my heart and focus my energy. It's a technique used by the samurai to avoid panic and fear before battle."

"I do something similar. Perhaps you can teach me your technique and I'll teach you mine." She sighed. "I never thought a youngster could teach me anything new."

We sat in companionable silence while she finished her tea. I studied the older woman out of the corners of my downcast eyes. Namika was sturdy with an extra layer of fat that kept the cold away from her bones in the sea, but her back rounded and the skin on her neck and jowls sagged.

"Namika, why do you still dive? You could retire, sit by a fire, and let the younger Ama care for you."

"Ask anyone." She snorted. "The best Ama are the older ones. We can stay in the cold sea and hold our breath longer than the younger girls." She looked over the water in silence.

I thought my question had offended her and prepared an apology.

"The sea calls to me. When I'm under the water, I'm in a magical kingdom." She swept her arm from head to foot. "It's who I am. I am Namika, 'flower of the wave.' Without the sea, I am nothing."

She looked at me with sad black eyes. "And you, Tokoyo? Why do you dive? You could stay in your father's fine house, have servants wait on you. Yet you are here risking death." She raised her bowl of tea. "And serving an old Ama."

Her question surprised me. I hadn't thought of why I learned the Ama trade. My father provided well for me. I had lovely clothes, good food, a warm house, and tutors. As his only child, he trained me as he would a son in fencing and other martial arts.

I delighted in his smile and lived for his praise, but I wanted more. Why?

"I think it's because it is something of my own." I let my gaze drift to the rippling waves. "I love my father and would do anything for him, but I dive for myself."

Namika patted my arm. "And it's adventurous. Most girls—even a samurai's daughter—don't get to cheat death, fight sharks, or find pearls of great worth."

"And it's adventurous." I agreed. "The gods blessed me with a loving father who indulges me in this."

"Few fathers would." She shrugged and looked at the setting sun. "And you should not test his patience by being late."

I bowed again to the wise Ama. "You're right. It's time, again, to become a nobleman's daughter."

Hana and the other Ama waved goodbye as I set off for the village of Shima and my father's estates.

4

FATHER'S HOME

THE GUARD SUPPRESSED A SCOWL as I entered the wooden gates carved with boars' heads. I don't think he approved of my father giving me so much freedom, but it was not his place to criticize my father's actions. I smiled sweetly and wished him a good day.

I inhaled the sweet scent of peach blossoms as I walked the winding path. Behind a screen of maples, I spied the red tile roof and wooden walls of our house. It was not the largest in the area, but not the smallest either. My ancestors had been samurai for generations. I'm sure it pained my father that he had no son to inherit his lands, but he never let me see his disappointment or made me feel less loved or esteemed.

I spied his horse being led to the stables and quickened my pace. I ran to the entryway, where servants removed my father's clogs and outer kimono.

"Father!" I shouted and launched myself into his arms.

"Tokoyo!" He grabbed me up and swung me around till my bandana fell off and my wet hair streamed down my back. "You've been diving today?" He set me on my feet, nearly breathless.

"Yes, Father. I found a pearl of great worth!" Blood flushed my cheeks from laughter and pride.

His eyes grew round. "Let's see this miraculous pearl."

"I uh...I uh..." I felt the blood drain from my face. *Should I have kept the pearl? It was valuable. Will father be angry with me for giving it away?* I squared my shoulders and faced him to receive whatever punishment he decreed. "I gave it to the Ama for teaching me their secrets."

"You did right, my child." His warm smile washed over me. "You should always pay your debts, especially to those poorer than you." He stopped, turned his head in the direction of the kitchen, and sniffed the air. "I think Cook has something special in store for us tonight. I smell duck spiced with *shiso*." He swatted my behind. "Go child, you need to bathe and dress for dinner."

"Yes, Father." I giggled and fled to my room. It was so good to have Father home!

5

A DEADLY CURSE

"QUICK, KIKO! I MUST BE READY SOON." My maid fussed with my hair until I was ready to take shears to my head. I was a maiden and needed only wear my hair down my back, loose or braided, but she insisted on adding combs and ribbons.

The most powerful man in Japan, Regent Hojo Takatoki, visited Shima today and Father accompanied him. I would be in the crowd and invisible to the Regent, but everyone dressed their best to honor the ruler of our country. At last Kiko helped me with my best silk kimono—white, decorated with dark pink cherry blossoms—and wound a red obi around my waist.

I tottered on my wooden clogs, weighed down by my silk robes, to the front door where a litter awaited me. I couldn't see past the heavy curtain and sweated in the still close air as we traveled to Shima. I soon heard the crowds as we entered the field where the Regent would speak. Children called to one another in high-pitched voices, people gossiped and complained about the hot sun, merchants called out their wares—cool drinks and sweet treats.

Because I was the daughter of a noble samurai, my bearers brought me to the front of the crowd. When they stopped, I stepped out into the sunshine to face a long shaded platform, higher than my head, draped in silk with a single gilded throne-like chair in the middle. Guards in full armor, swords drawn, ringed the platform. There were no steps at the front or sides, so anyone getting onto the platform must go up the back.

My bearers took the litter away, but a crowd of servants attended me. One shaded me with a parasol. Two others offered me chilled juice and honeyed nuts. I nodded to the other noble ladies I knew from the area, all equally well-attended.

A string of nobles and advisors stepped between the drapes on the platform and took positions around the throne. The closer to the chair, the more important the person. Father stood two men away and my heart swelled with pride that he was so well-thought of at court. A trumpeter joined the throng and blasted for attention. When the crowd quieted, he announced, "The people of Shima, bow to the Regent Hojo Takatoki."

We all went to our knees and bowed our heads to the ground. Servants brought the Regent onto the stage in a litter and helped him to his seat. The trumpeter led a series of acclamations which lasted for several minutes, then he gave us permission to rise. No one sat in the Regent's presence.

I was surprised at the Regent's appearance. Younger than my father, he seemed much older. Gray speckled his hair and mustaches. Deep bruises shadowed his eyes. His skin was yellowish and cheeks hollow. Father had always talked of the Regent as vigorous, but this man suffered from an obvious illness. A barely perceptible murmur swept through the crowd as others saw what I did. The Regent's sons were young. His death would likely lead to rebellion and civil war—an outcome no one wanted.

The trumpeter blasted again and the whispers ceased.

An older man, standing to the Regent's right came forward carrying a scroll. He unwound it and read:

"I, Regent Hojo Takatoki, ask my good servant and First Minister Ichijô Uchitsune to read my words, because I am unable. Several weeks ago, I was struck down with a sickness. Demons haunt my dreams and I cannot sleep. The best physicians can find no physical reason for this and fear I have been cursed."

The crowd gasped and murmured. Curses were dangerous and fearsome things—not as bad as vengeful ghosts, but nearly!

"After careful investigation we have found the traitor in our midst." The First Minister took a dramatic pause.

The crowd cried, "Name the traitor! Death to the traitor!"

The minister smiled, curled the scroll, and pointed at my father. "Guards take the samurai Oribe Shima into custody!"

6

ARRESTED

MY MIND SWIRLED IN CONFUSION as the crowd stilled in shock. *My beloved father, a traitor?*

Father turned pale and dropped to his knees. "Honored Regent, I am innocent of this charge. I would never seek to harm you!"

The crowd erupted, shouting and asking questions, because Father was much beloved in the area.

"Silence!" the minister thundered.

The crowd quieted. My heart thudded with fear.

"Oribe Shima is banished to the Oki Islands by order of the Regent. This is done as a warning to anyone who threatens our sovereignty or our person. His lands and fortune are forfeit."

What was happening? How could anyone believe my father guilty of such deeds?

"I demand to know who accuses me of such a crime. With what evidence?" Father shouted as guards pulled him to his feet.

"Father!" I screamed.

He didn't hear me in all the confusion. The guards led him to the back stairs. I picked up my skirts, kicked off my clogs and ran to the back.

The guards strong-armed Father down the rear steps.

I pushed my way past one and fell, grabbing my father's knees and sobbing.

Pain shot through my scalp as one of the guards grabbed me by the hair and tried to pull me away. I clung tighter, trying to keep my world from falling apart.

Another guard kicked me in the side and I gasped. Father twisted free and threw his body over mine to shield me from further harm.

"Tokoyo, my child," he whispered. "You must be brave." He grunted as a guard beat him with a staff. "Stop," he shouted. "A moment with my daughter. Please! I will come with you willingly."

The beating stopped.

"Go home. Gather what valuables you can. Go to our steward. He will shelter you for loyalty's sake. I'll send word when I can." He kissed my wet cheeks. "Be a brave samurai's daughter. Make me proud. Go now."

Father stood up and helped me to my feet. He hugged me tight and whispered into my hair. "I love you."

"I love you, too, Father." I wiped the tears from my cheeks and stood tall. "I'll do all I can to free you."

"Enough." One beefy guard grabbed my elbow and swung me away. Two more bound my father's arms and marched him down the path.

My heart nearly broke as I watched him go. What was I to do now?

7

A THIEVING CLERK

I ARRIVED HOME to find all in confusion. Imperial guards stood at the gate. Servants streamed out wailing. Did the Regent intend to turn them out to starve in the countryside?

I glided up to a guard in my best demure lady manner and spoke mildly, "Please, Kind Sir, who is in charge? I am the daughter of the house and would speak with him."

I must have looked pitiful with my torn clothes, mussed hair, and tear-stained cheeks. He escorted me inside to an officious-looking clerk, a bald man with long mustaches and ink-stained fingers scribbling in a ledger at my father's low desk.

I approached, head bowed, hands clasped in front of me, hidden by the long sleeves of my kimono. "Honored Sir, I understand you have been appointed the new steward of this house?"

He nodded and looked up, squinting through near-sighted eyes. "Yes, I'm here on behalf of my master the First Minister."

I stifled a gasp. The man who most benefitted from my father's fall was likely the one who falsely accused him. The First Minister of the land might be an impossible opponent. I bobbed my head. "Chief Steward, I am the daughter of the house and came to collect my possessions."

"The Regent declared Oribe Shima's land and fortune forfeit to my master."

"I understand, Honored Sir, but he did not claim my possessions. I have some poor baubles my mother left me." I let a tear track my cheek. "She died giving birth to my still-born brother when I was little more than a babe."

He frowned and continued making notes.

Appealing to his kind heart didn't seem to work. I tried another tactic. "I have little of worth, but I would be happy to gift you with my most valuable piece for allowing me to take what is mine." I looked around at the lacquered furniture and delicate scroll paintings on the walls of my home. "It seems a shame you work so hard for your esteemed master and enjoy no special reward."

"Well, the decree didn't mention any of your possessions." His lips curled in a smile that did not reach his eyes. "Show me what you've got."

I led him down the hall to my room and pulled the screen aside. A sob tightened my chest at the familiar sights: my sleeping mat covered with silk pillows, an ink drawing of a mountain and birds hanging on the wall, a small shrine in the corner with copper bowl and incense sticks, a black lacquered chest containing my valuables. I opened the chest first, pulled out a small carved box, and showed the clerk the contents.

This time the smile was real. "Lovely." He fingered a matching jade necklace and earrings.

While he rummaged through my jewels, I made a small pack. My silks would do me little good out in the world. I packed my training clothes, sturdy leather sandals, a warm cloak, and a silk kerchief my mother had embroidered with a red bird. It smelled faintly of her favorite jasmine scent. I turned to see the clerk admiring my favorite piece: a gold brooch shaped like a dragon.

"Have you decided?"

"Yes." He picked up the box. "I'll take it all."

"And leave me with nothing?" My mouth dropped. "How will I survive?"

"Not my problem." He noticed a knife with an intricately carved hilt mounted on the wall. "You can take the knife. If life gets too desperate, you can make good use of it." He laughed. "After all, you're a traitorous samurai's daughter. The world would be better cleansed of such scum as you and your traitor father."

My shoulders stiffened, but I bowed my head in submission. He was right that the knife could be used in ritual suicide, but that's not why I wanted it.

8

HOMELESS

I TOOK THE KNIFE down from the wall and added it to my meager pack. The greedy steward had given me the most precious thing in the room: my many-times-great ancestor's knife. The blessings carved into the hilt had special powers for anyone of my blood. I had wondered how I would smuggle it out of the room and the steward solved my problem.

Outside the gate, the servants were gone; off to their families' or friends' homes.

It hit me: I had nowhere to go.

I was an outcast among the noble class. No one would cross the First Minister to take me in—not even our former servants. I had no money to rent a room or buy food. I had no relatives. I was completely alone.

I sat on a grassy bank and cried—great wracking sobs—grieving for my lost life.

I reached into my pack for my diving bandana. As I blew my nose, the solution came to me. The Ama! No one would look for me among the diving women. I could earn my own keep and maybe save a coin or two until I figured out how to rescue Father.

I gathered my things and headed for the *amagoya*.

* * * * *

"Tokoyo?" Hana squinted at me standing in the shadows "Is that you?"

"Yes." I bowed my head. "May I come in?"

"Of course!" She backed away from the door and let me pass, taking note of my bedraggled appearance. "I was worried about you after the Regent, ah, you know."

Tears tightened my throat and I swallowed. "I have nowhere else to go. Can I stay with the Ama until I figure out what to do?"

She pulled me into a hug. "You are welcome to stay as long as you like."

I looked around the rambling *amagoya* the

Ama shared until they married. Because they brought in extra cash during the diving season, my friends were sought after as brides and could take their time and choose their husbands.

Namika sat on a tatami mat in the corner dozing.

When the door shut, the old woman snorted and woke. She blinked at me. "Tokoyo?"

"Yes." I approached and kneeled at her feet.

"Poor child." She leaned forward and patted my head. "I'm glad you came to us. We take care of our own."

Gratitude flooded my body with warmth. I was not alone.

But Father was.

9

LIFE WITH THE AMA

THE SUMMER MONTHS proved satisfying. The winter months less so. I dove every day of the season with the Ama. My body grew strong swimming, diving, and hauling the catch. During the stormy winter, I learned the household arts of cleaning, cooking, and mending as I took my turns in the communal house.

I heard nothing from or about Father. I paid the inn keeper a hard-earned string of *kochosen* copper coins to let me know if any messengers came asking for me.

Nothing.

One day, as spring drew closer, I stood on the porch looking out to sea at a brewing storm. The clouds towered over the horizon, filled with the same darkness and bitter lightning that filled my soul. I dithered here in safety and relative comfort while my father wasted away on a barren island. I needed to do something, but what?

After our dinner of rice and fish, I sat brooding, looking into the fire. The storm raged around us rattling the window shutters and whistling under the eaves. The sky *Kami*—storm spirits—must have been angry.

I know I was.

Angry at the foul man who ruined my father. Angry at myself for being a helpless girl. Angry at my father for going away...even though it wasn't his fault.

The bitter feeling soured my stomach. A pain shot through my middle and I moaned.

"Are you alright, child?" Namika stood at my shoulder.

I stiffened, not wanting her to know my weakness. "I'm fine."

She folded her aging body into a sitting position on the floor while holding two bowls of steaming tea. Many younger women couldn't do that. "Does your stomach bother you?"

"A little."

"When you keep bad feelings inside, you feed the demons." She handed me a bowl of tea.

I sniffed. Ginger, spearmint, and a bitter herb I couldn't identify sweetened with honey. Probably an old remedy. "Thanks." I took a sip. The warmth travelled down my throat to my stomach. Two more sips relaxed me.

"Now tell me what troubles you so." A boom of thunder rattled the shutters and I startled. Namika looked at me through half-lidded eyes. "It's not the storm. You've lived through worse."

"I miss my father." A sudden sob choked my throat. I had thought I was angry, but sadness overwhelmed me. "We've never been apart this long. I don't know if he's alive or dead!"

"What does your heart tell you?"

"He said he'd send word. He must be dead."

There.

I said it out loud.

My greatest fear.

Father was dead and I'd never see him again. I'd be forever alone in this world. Grief closed my throat and I put the tea on the floor until I could recover.

"Hmmm. I can think of several reasons you've heard nothing." The old woman counted off on her fingers, "He is guarded too closely to send a message. His messenger took his money and didn't deliver the message. His messenger was killed, injured, or otherwise delayed on the way. The messenger can't find you…"

"The messenger can't find me!" I snapped my fingers. "Of course! Father told me to go to our steward's. He has no way of knowing that I was turned out with nothing and sought shelter with the Ama."

Hope lifted my soul. *Father wasn't dead. He hadn't abandoned me! And I must not abandon him.*

"I must go to him."

Namika widened her eyes. "Are you sure? That is a dangerous journey across the mountains and the sea."

"I must find my father and share his exile. We can be a comfort to each other." I lowered my head and a tear dropped on my knee. "I miss him so much!"

"Of course you do, child." Namika enclosed me in a warm embrace. "But I thought you wanted to clear your father's name."

"I had hoped to, but look how I've spent my time. Surviving. I have no friends at court. I have no hope of finding the evidence that the First Minister framed my father." The injustice of it stung my pride, but I saw little I could do. "I'm a young girl and the minister is a powerful man. If I ever want to see my father again, I must join him in exile."

"You're determined on this course?"

I nodded, feeling light now that I had made this decision.

"Then tomorrow we go to the market and get you traveling supplies." Namika patted my hand.

"I have little money left from my share of the diving season." I frowned. "How much will it take to travel the mountains and the sea?"

"Do you have anything to sell or barter?"

"The silks I came in."

"Nothing else?"

I thought of my ancestor's knife and my mother's silk kerchief and shook my head. I would never part with either, even if I starved.

"I have a surprise for you." Namika smiled and pulled a small bag of coins from her belt. "This is your share from the pearl of great worth you found early last season."

"But I gifted that to you and the other Ama!"

"We all thought it fair you have a share of the pearl you found. I've been saving it for you, knowing you would have great need of it, if you left us." She pressed the bag into my hands. "This will get you to your father, if you're frugal."

I threw my arms around the old woman and hugged her tight "Thank you, Honored Grandmother."

She laughed and pushed me away. "Don't break these old bones. I plan on diving for many more years."

10

FINDING A BOAT

I ARRIVED AT THE VILLAGE OF AKASAKI on the northern coast during the late afternoon, footsore and nearly out of money. It had taken me most of the spring to travel over the mountains and west to this small fishing village, so like my home village of Shima. I hurried to the beach where fishermen and their families pulled their boats from the water, sorted their catch, and mended nets. If I squinted, I could see the tops of misty mountains on the Oki Islands across the sea.

My heart soared at being so close to my father.

I approached the first fisherman I met: a skinny man with crooked teeth and kind eyes.

"Please, Kind Sir, how much would you charge to take me to the Oki Islands?"

He frowned and looked me over. "No one will take you to the Okis. It's forbidden."

"Forbidden? Why?"

"I don't know for sure." He shrugged. "Since they banished the Emperor Go-Toba to the Okis in my grandfather's time, we haven't been allowed ashore."

"But I've come such a long way. I need to get to the islands," I wailed, my voice cracking.

"I'm sorry, Miss."

I squared my shoulders. He wasn't the only fisherman in the village.

By the time I reached the end of the beach, my shoulders slumped with disappointment. No man would ferry me across for any amount of money. I sat on a rock looking out to sea. Father was so close! I had to find a way.

"Miss?"

I looked up at a young man, whose handsome face was marred by a purple birthmark shaped like a baby's fist on his right cheek. A sign of bad luck.

"You want to go to the Oki Islands?"

"Yes." After so much failure, I was cautious. "Can you help me?"

"Possibly." His eyes glittered. "How much money do you have?"

His question raised the hairs on the back of

my neck. There were rules to bargaining and he just broke one. "I like to know the name of the people I do business with."

"Nijo." He put a hand on his chest and bowed. He straightened. "Do you want to go or not? You can pay me half now and the rest when we get there."

He didn't ask my name or my story, like the others. All he was interested in was my money. "Why would you do this when no one else will?"

"They're all cowards; afraid of the Regent's agents." He thumped his chest. "I'm the best sailor in the village. Ask anyone!" Nijo swept his hand across the horizon. "And I have the best boat!" This time he pointed to a shabby boat—the smallest on the beach.

"I haven't much money." I named half my stash, a plan beginning to form in my mind.

"It's not much." He frowned and seemed to reconsider, stroking his chin. "But to help a young girl, I could be persuaded. Give me all the money now and meet me here tomorrow morning. I'll take you to the Okis."

I pulled a string of copper *kochosen* coins from my purse and handed them over.

"Good." Nijo grinned. "Tomorrow morning.

First light." He strode down the beach toward a ramshackle tavern that served the fishermen.

I followed. I needed to get into the village and buy food for the trip.

"I hope you didn't give Uda any money." The first fisherman with the kind eyes said as I walked past. "I saw him talking to you. He's lazy and a cheat."

Uda? So the man intended to cheat me and gave me a false name so I couldn't accuse him. I watched Uda shove the tavern door open, roaring for a drink. Knowing his true nature made me more determined in my plan and my honor remained unstained.

"I won't be doing any business with Uda." My stomach rumbled. "Where can I buy food and find a room for the night?"

The fisherman gave me directions to the market where I used the last of my money to buy noodles for dinner and rice balls for my travel. I didn't take a room.

After the sun set and the moon rose, I went back to the beach. The waves rippled on the stony shore in that calm time when the breezes died. I walked the beach until I came to Uda's small boat. It was the only one I could handle alone. I threw my pack into the bottom, untied the boat from its moorings, and pulled it into deeper water, where I climbed aboard.

"Thanks for the use of your boat, Uda!" I smiled as I rowed the boat toward the islands on the horizon. "I'll bring it back if I can."

11

THE OKI ISLANDS

BY DAYBREAK, I WAS EXHAUSTED, with blistered hands and aching back. I had thought myself strong from the diving and traveling, but rowing used entirely different muscles. I stopped to chew a rice ball and drink tea from my flask. Lights from Atasaki blinked on the horizon.

I wondered if Uda staggered to the beach looking bewildered at the empty spot where his boat used to be. More likely he stayed at home hiding from me, pleased with his cleverness.

I felt a small pang of guilt for taking his boat, even if I did pay for it. What made one man noble and kind and another a liar and a cheat? Was the mark on Uda's face a sign of his nature or did the disfigurement cause others to treat him as a cheat, so he became one?

I shrugged and stretched my shoulders.

Wondering on the nature of Uda would not get me closer to the islands.

To the north, the Oki Islands loomed dark and forbidding. As the sun rose, I saw the deep forests coming down to the shore. Which island held my father? How would I find him?

I shook my head. I had to get there first.

I wrapped my blistered hands in scraps of cloth and started to row. I could feel a current tugging me along and blessed Funadama for helping me.

By midafternoon, I reached the first island, but found no place to come ashore. The sea dashed against steep cliffs and jumbles of large boulders. I rowed further; passing more forbidding shores until I came to the largest island the furthest north. I almost despaired of finding any safe place to land when I noticed a flock of terns winging their way to a narrow stony beach, just visible at high tide.

I rowed to the shore, pulled the boat onto the beach and tied it to a boulder. So tired my bones ached, I took my pack to a sheltered spot, ate the last of my rice, wrapped myself in my warm cloak, and fell asleep. I dreamed of my father. When I found him, he laughed and lifted me into his strong arms, swinging me around. I felt safe and loved.

A cold salty breeze woke me. My stomach growled and I drank the last of my tea. I considered taking the boat out to dive for food, but I didn't know the waters. How deep were they? How swift the current? Were there sharks, giant squid, or stinging jellyfish? *Best to go hungry for a while.*

I packed my meager things, stuck my ancestor's knife in my belt and searched for a way off the beach. I found a faint steep track at one end and started climbing the wet difficult path. Twisted salt-sprayed shrubs gave way to wind-blown pines. I reached the top of the bluff and followed the rim down a valley, until I came to a meandering stream.

I knelt on the mossy bank to drink and wash my face. I filled my flask and followed the stream. It led me to a small fishing hamlet nestled on the shore where the stream met the sea. My pace quickened at the smell of smoke and drying seaweed.

At last!

Hope bloomed in my chest.

Father, I'm coming for you!

12

THE SEARCH BEGINS

I ENTERED THE HAMLET of nine huts to find the men out to sea. The women washed clothes and dried fish. An older girl looked after a gaggle of children who ran screeching through the village. When the children spied me coming down the path, they ran back to their mothers. Some clutched their mother's skirts and stuck their thumbs in their mouths. Others–more bold–turned to look me over. One offered a shy smile.

I walked up to the oldest woman–a bent crone, with wispy white hair, sitting on a bench, spinning sheep's wool into yarn–and bowed. "Honored Grandmother, I am Tokoyo, daughter of the samurai Oribe Shima. I've come to find my father who was banished to the Oki Islands by the Regent Hojo Takatoki. Do you have any knowledge of where they keep the banished ones?"

"Shima? You've come a long way, child." She looked up at me, squinting.

My stomach rumbled and blood rushed to my face in embarrassment.

"And you're hungry." She snapped her fingers at a matronly woman. "Daughter-in-law, bring this child food." The woman scowled and ducked into a hut. "Suki is a good wife to my son. She gave him many children, but she is anxious for me to die so she can run the household." The old woman chuckled. "Now tell me your story."

I told the old woman of my father's false imprisonment, my life with the Ama, and my determination to find my father.

Suki appeared with rice soup flavored with fish broth, and two bowls of tea. "Honored Mother-in-law, may I get you anything else?"

The old woman waved her away. The other women turned back to their tasks which seemed to require them to move closer to me and the matriarch. She ignored them, but I smiled and nodded when I caught them staring at me. They probably didn't get many strangers in their hamlet.

"You dove with the Ama, did you?" The old woman slurped her tea. "I always wanted to learn that trade, but the waters around these islands are not suitable–too deep."

I reined in my impatience and we chatted about the sea and fishing for several minutes. Finally, I could wait no longer. I put down my tea. "Thank you for the food and kind company, but I must be on my way. Is there nothing you can tell me about where I might find my father?"

The old woman frowned.

I hoped I hadn't offended her.

She turned a sharp eye on the loitering women and whispered. "It is forbidden to talk of the missing ones. If word reaches the Regent's agents that someone is asking after a prisoner, they may fear escape and kill your father. If you value his life, don't ask after him."

"But how will I find him?" I whispered back in despair.

"Talk of other things: where the boats go; who is buying the catch. Look for men who have money, but don't seem to work at any trade. They'll be the guards."

"Thank you, Honored Grandmother. You are wise and generous." I bowed to the old woman. My task had become much harder, but I could accomplish it. "Can you tell me how to get to the next village?"

13

HARD TIMES

I FOLLOWED THE OLD WOMAN'S ADVICE, but learned nothing. Every hamlet I visited was much like the last: the men fished, the women washed and cleaned, the children played. No one sold their catch off the island. No boats made mysterious trips to other villages or islands.

I grew hungry and thin. I offered to work for food. Some people were kind and gave me scraps. Other's sent me off with a kick or threat. On the edge of starvation, I traded my good wool cloak and other clothes for food, until I had nothing but the rags on my back, my mother's kerchief and my ancestor's knife.

I lost track of the days, but it felt like midsummer when I reached the end of my strength and fell into despair. Father was nowhere on this island. I had tramped every inch of it. He must be on one of the smaller islands to the south and I had no way of knowing which, much less finding a way to get to him. I had no money to buy passage, even if a boat went there. Uda's boat was long gone: smashed to driftwood by the waves. I didn't have the strength to manage the larger fishing boats from the villages—even if I could honorably steal one.

I hiked to the south. At the end of a long day, tired and beyond hungry, I found myself on a bluff overlooking the sea. Gulls cried to one another as they flew in graceful circles. The southern Oki Islands, shrouded in mist, loomed beyond narrow straits. A swift current roiled the waves, but I saw a quiet cove below me with a narrow beach to the left. An overgrown path led from the bluff to the beach.

Bitterness at fate and anger at my failure gripped me, but I was too tired and hungry to cry. I sat on a boulder looking out to sea, my mind drifting back to more pleasant times: my father smiling at me as I fenced, his warm embrace when he returned from the capital, the camaraderie of the Ama after a long day diving. The dreams were so real I could feel the stubble on my father's face as he kissed me and smell the fish the Ama prepared for lunch.

The raucous cry of an albatross brought me back to the present. I shivered, longing to return to the comfort of my dreams, but the emptiness of my stomach and the sorrow in my soul won out.

"Father, forgive me," I whispered to the wind. "I have failed and see no way forward."

I would go to the beach below and swim for the far shore. I knew I had little chance of making the other island, given my weakness and the choppy currents. But trying and failing was better than dying of starvation on the shore.

I took two steps toward the path, when I noticed a small shrine under a mulberry tree twisted by the constant wind. Thinking to plead for the favor of my ancestors, I approached. A copper bowl, flanked with incense holders, topped a plain wooden altar. I had no food to sacrifice or sweet smelling joss sticks to burn. I bowed to the altar, pulled my knife from my belt, and presented it in both hands.

"Honored Ancestors, send me strength and wisdom. I have failed to find my father or clear his name. I am a daughter of your line and the last of your name. Please give me strength to do the honorable thing."

The hilt with the blessings warmed in my hand. I looked at it and the glyphs seemed to move and dance. I rubbed my eyes. I felt an overwhelming need to sleep.

"Thank you," I mumbled and curled up, eyes closing.

14

THE SACRIFICE

"NAMU AMIDA BUTSU" Clap. Clap. *"Namu Amida Butsu"* Clap. Clap. *"Namu Amida Butsu"* Clap. Clap.

I woke from a deep and dreamless sleep, startled by the Buddhist chant and clapping. I sat up and looked through the mulberry tree. The full moon shone down on two people, dressed in white. An old man in priestly robes chanted and clapped while a young girl, her hair hanging loose around her shoulders, kneeled at his feet, sobbing.

The priest reached down and took the girl by the hand. He led her to the edge of the cliff overlooking the cove. She struggled crying, "No! Please! I don't want to die!"

I jumped up and ran to the cliff before I could think. I grabbed the girl and pulled her away from the edge. I sheltered her with my body, knife drawn. Strength seemed to flow from the hilt. My heart thudded with the action.

"Leave her alone, you monster!" I cried.

The priest stared at me, eyes round, mouth open in surprise. He crossed his arms, put his hands in his sleeves, and bowed to me.

"You have it wrong. I am not the monster here. I do my duty–horrible as it is. It gives me no pleasure to end the life of another." He gazed at the girl cowering behind me and tears filled his eyes. "A demon named Yofune-Nushi lives in the sea below. He demands a sacrifice from us each year in June on the Day of the Dog. One of our young people under the age of sixteen must be thrown into the sea between moonrise and moonset. If he is not appeased, he attacks our fishing fleet with sudden and terrible storms. So you see, we sacrifice one to save many."

The girl crouched behind me, trembling, clutching my knees. I gently untangled her. "Is this true?"

"Yes. I lost the lottery. I know I should be brave. I'm saving the lives of many good men, my father and brother among them, but..." Her lips trembled. "But...I'm so scared!" She fell into my arms weeping.

I patted her back as she sobbed.

The priest looked at the full moon as it lowered in the sky. "We must continue the sacrifice."

The girl's shoulders stiffened. She pushed away from me and wiped the tears from her cheeks. She took a deep shaky breath. "I'm ready now."

"No!"

"I can do this." She laid a gentle hand on my arm. "For my father and brother."

"Let me be the sacrifice."

The words tumbled out before I realized what I said. When I heard them, I knew they were right. I could die honorably with purpose and possibly—*just possibly*—survive with the gratitude of the island for saving them from a monster.

"You have a family that loves you. My father is lost to me. I have no home, no family, nothing to live for. I had planned to swim into the sea. Let my sacrifice be for something. Let me save you."

The girl looked over my shoulder at the priest, hope shining in her eyes.

I turned to see the old man nodding. "Are you sure?"

"Yes." My voice rang with confidence. "I am a samurai's daughter and trained Ama. If I'm lucky, I will kill the demon and break the curse on your land. If I'm not..." I shrugged my shoulders. "I can die an honorable death to save this girl and free your village for another year."

"What is your name, Brave One, so we may honor your sacrifice?"

"Tokoyo, daughter of samurai Oribe Shima."

"Tokoyo, daughter of Oribe Shima, you do your father much honor." He bowed to me. "Take the white robe of sacrifice. We will pray for your success."

I tore off my rags and put the girl's white robe over my Ama's loincloth, my knife secured with a long sash. I tied my bandana around my hair, grateful for the extra blessings printed on the cloth.

"I want you to have this." I tucked the silk kerchief into the girl's hand. "It belonged to my mother."

"I'll keep it for your return." She clasped my hand and whispered. "Thank you, Tokoyo. Be brave. We will wait for you."

I walked to the edge of the cliff and looked down at the still water. Touching the hilt of my knife, I again felt its power.

I could do this.

I smiled at the old priest and the girl, took a deep breath, and dove off the cliff.

15

A DEMON IN THE DEEP

THE WIND RUSHED BY ME and I knifed through the calm surface with barely a splash. The momentum took me deep. I cut through the cold water like a spear, leaving a trail of bubbles behind. The full moon lit the water like a distant lamp, shimmering on the rocks and small schools of fish. I swam for the bottom, alert for the demon.

I didn't find him.

I swam deeper.

No sign of Yofune-Nushi.

My lungs began to ache. I knew I couldn't make it back to the surface even with my samurai and Ama training.

Was this for nothing?

Below me light spilled onto a sandy bottom. I swam deeper and saw a cave with light streaming past the figure of a man seated on the sand.

How could that be?

I swam toward the figure, thinking it might be the demon, and entered the cave.

As I got closer I realized it was a wooden statue and looked up. Light shimmered off a surface, several feet above me. I pushed off from the bottom and broke through to a pocket of air trapped in the cave. I let my breath out in a slow whistle, gulped a lungful of air, and stared.

The cave stretched for many yards. The ceiling and walls pulsed with light, as if they were alive. When I ran my hands through the water, they left a trail of blinking lights, like tiny stars. I had never seen anything like it. I looked down at the sandy bottom of the cave, curious about the statue. I dove down, pulled it up into the air, and placed it on a rocky shelf above the opening.

The face looked familiar.

I studied it in the dim light and realized it was a likeness of the Regent!

Anger coursed through my veins like hot lead. If I couldn't destroy the demon, I could obliterate the image of the man who banished my father and caused all my misery.

I grabbed my knife and raised it to strike the hated image.

An inscription on the side of the statue caught my eye.

I narrowed my eyes to read it in the dim light: "Ichijô Uchitsune curses Hojo Takatoki. May his dreams be filled with death and his waking plagued with fear. May he never rest again until he is in his grave."

I gasped. The curse was real! I had the proof that my father was innocent. I held the hilt of my knife to my forehead and closed my eyes, "Bless you Honored Ancestors for leading me here. I will not fail to free my father." Warmth and strength spread from my head to my toes.

I tied the statue to me with the sash, took a deep breath, and dove for the cave entrance.

A long figure swam past the entrance. *An eel? They could be dangerous.* I swam closer and looked out.

Yofune-Nushi!

When the demon had not attacked me, I thought the villagers mistaken, but he swam back and forth across the entrance. Iridescent scales covered his dragon-like body and a spiny fin ran down his backbone. Tiny legs with wicked claws ringed a body five times the length of mine. But the most horrible part was the head.

Yofune-Nushi's long snout bristled with razor sharp teeth. His eyes, perched on the top of his head, glowed a demonic unblinking red.

He looked right at me.

I froze.

16

A FIGHT TO THE DEATH

THE MONSTER WHIPPED ITS TAIL and swam toward me, jaws wide to swallow me whole.

Time seemed to slow, as I tensed my body for battle. I released the knot in my sash and let the statue fall to the bottom. My knife glowed.

Yofune-Nushi rushed at me.

At the last second I darted to the side and struck him in the eye.

The demon screamed with rage and pain, the sound distorted by the water. He thrashed and stirred the bloody water with sand.

It was getting hard to see in the murk, and my lungs ached for air. I stroked for the surface of the cave, took a long breath, and dove again to do battle.

The demon waited for me at the entrance, his one eye glaring balefully.

This time I didn't wait, but swam at his blind

side and struck between his head and the base of his spiny fin. My knife slid off the scales and I nearly pierced my own thigh. The shock of the blocked blow numbed my arm.

Yofune-Nushi turned, swift as an eel, snapping at my legs.

I kicked hard at his nose, as I would a shark, and caught him a sharp blow.

He recoiled and swam above me, cutting me off from the surface...and exposing his belly.

I kicked off from the sandy bottom with all my force, swimming straight for the beast's tender underside.

I plunged my knife up to the hilt into his heart.

Yofune-Nushi thrashed in pain ripping the knife from my grip. He snapped at the blade, but his frantic actions became slower and slower.

His toothed snout opened, releasing bubbles and blood, as he slowly drifted to the bottom. I watched as the fire died from his one good eye.

I stroked for the surface.

I broke through to air, whistled, and breathed deep. I swam to the ledge and pulled myself up, shaking like an aspen leaf.

I did it! I killed Yofune-Nushi and had the evidence to free my father.

I sat, head on knees, teetering between laughing in triumph and crying in relief. My gargled sounds echoed off the cave walls and subsided into hiccups.

The battle strength drained away and I shivered from the cold. I needed to get the statue to the surface and find a way to bring it to the Regent. If the First Minister found out I had the proof of his guilt, he would try to stop me; maybe kill Father.

And what of Yofune-Nushi? Would the villagers believe me without proof of his death? They might keep sacrificing children for nothing!

Weak and cold, I reached for my knife, hoping for more strength. When my hand grasped empty air, I sat open-mouthed for a moment. Then I remembered: it was stuck in the heart of the demon.

I licked the salty water from my lips and stood. I wouldn't leave my knife, the statue, or the demon on the bottom of the sea. I would find the strength to bring all to the surface.

I closed my eyes and settled my mind, using the exercises I learned at my father's knee. With one last deep breath I dove to the bottom of the cave. With swift moves, I tied the statue to my waist, hoisted the demon to my shoulder, and swam for the entrance.

The moon provided a glowing path to the surface and I kicked with all my might. The sodden statue and dead demon were lighter in the water than in the air, but they still weighed me down. I had to push myself to the top, muscles aching with the strain.

The shimmering moon blurred and wavered before my eyes, but never seemed to grow any closer.

I had to be near the surface. I couldn't fail now that I had come so far.

My lungs burned like fire. My arms and legs felt heavy as lead.

I could drop the statue and demon and save myself...but only a few more yards...

Darkness crept into the edges of my sight. My heart thudded painfully.

Father, it would be so easy to let go...give up...let the sea take me.

Bubbles dribbled from my nose as my body screamed for air.

So close...So close...

Blackness.

A GRATEFUL VILLAGE

"TOKOYO! TOKOYO!"

Father?

I woke, lying on my side on a rocky beach, coughing and spitting. Salt water burned my throat and nose.

I took a ragged gasp of blessed fresh air.

The old priest thumped my back. When I spit up the last of the sea water, he sat back on his heels.

The girl sat rubbing my feet and grinned at me. "Thank the *Kami*, Tokoyo! You survived!"

Both priest and girl were soaked up to their waists.

"We saw you struggling to the surface from the beach and came to help." The priest nodded towards the edge of the beach. The statue lay toppled on the shore and the demon sprawled half in and half out of the gentle lapping waves.

"Thank you." I sat up. The world tilted and spun. I shut my eyes and put my head on my knees until the world settled. When I opened my eyes the second time, everything stayed in place.

Then it struck me: I survived! Father would be freed!

I wanted to jump up and shout to the moon, but I had no strength to laugh or cry much less jump around. I could only sigh.

I heard the priest and girl whispering, then the girl left to climb the path.

"I sent her for help. We cannot carry you and you're in no condition to walk any distance. Let me help you to a more comfortable place."

He helped me stand and we hobbled to a sheltered sandy spot. As we passed the body of the demon, I remembered. "My knife! Can you get it from the demon's body?"

I leaned against a boulder as the old man shoved over the monster and pulled my knife from its heart. I had a momentary fear that, with the knife gone, Yofune-Nushi might come back to life, but the monster took no breath, no fire lit its eye.

"Thank you, again." The priest handed me the knife hilt first.

This time there was no heat, no strength. It must only work in times of great need. I sat in the soft sand, back to the cliff and promptly fell asleep.

* * * * *

"Tokoyo." The priest shook my shoulder gently. "Child, they're coming."

The short rest renewed me. I stood up. Several men snaked down the path from the bluff, carrying torches and small bundles.

The girl waved at me and rushed to my side with a basket. "Tea and rice cakes!"

I drank the bracing tea from a flask and wolfed down the rice cakes soaked in honey. No banquet in my father's hall had tasted so good.

When was the last time I ate?

It didn't matter.

The men milled around the demon's body, talking excitedly and pointing. A tall man, his face darkened by the sun and the sea, came over and bowed to me. "I'm Toba, Ena's father." He nodded to the girl. "I'm forever indebted to you for saving her life and killing the demon. She told me you have no family. I would be honored to give you a home and call you daughter."

The offer brought a lump to my throat and tears to my eyes. I bowed my head. "Thank you. Your offer is generous and touches me deeply, but I can now restore my father's good name and be reunited with him." I pointed at the statue. "That figure of the Regent is cursed and causes his current illness, but I'll need help. I must get word to the Regent, without alerting the First Minister who cast the curse."

"The governor of our island has a feud with the minister. He will help you."

My smile almost cracked my face.

"But first we must get you back to the village and fatten you up." Toba looked me over and clucked like a mother hen. "My good wife will take care of you." He turned to the men. "Pack up the statue and the demon's body. Back to the village for a celebration!"

They all cheered and set to work.

For the first time since I left the Ama, I knew all would be well.

18

REVENGE

I KNOCKED ON THE DOOR of the *amagoya* much later than I planned. I should have stayed at the village inn with the Oki Island governor's men, but I wanted to see my friends and let them know I was safe.

Hana opened the door, rubbing sleep from her eyes and holding a lamp high. "Tokoyo?" She gaped at me, eyes wide. "Are you a ghost?"

"No. I'm flesh." I held out my hand for her clasp. She took it in her own and ran her thumb over the calluses on my palm.

Her face lit up with a smile. "You're real! We heard nothing for months and feared the worst."

"It almost was the worst." I shivered at the memories of the cold water and the demon's red eyes. "But I succeeded. I freed my father."

"You're cold. Don't stand there in the door. Come in and tell us all that's happened to you." Hana ushered me into the common room.

Sleepy Ama rose from their mats, lit lamps, and started hot water for tea. Namika sat in the middle, cross-legged, her gray hair in a messy braid over her shoulder. "Come, child. Sit by me and tell us of your adventures." She patted the mat next to her.

I folded myself onto the spot and took a deep breath. Namika smelled of the sea—salty brine and fresh air. Hana thrust a cup of hot tea into my hands. I took a sip. "It is a long story with many setbacks..." I launched into my tale dropping into the rhythms of a story teller. The Ama laughed when I outsmarted Uda, moaned when I starved, gasped at my battle with the demon, and cheered my success.

"I have one more task: reclaim my father's estate from the greedy steward who robbed me of my mother's jewelry and turned me out of my home penniless."

"If you need any help, there are many in the countryside who would see this man brought low." Namika frowned. "He squeezed everyone for taxes, leaving many next to starvation. Even we Ama barely made enough to live on, much less send money to our families."

The other Ama muttered, scowled, and nodded their heads.

"Good! The governor of the Oki Islands sent men with me. The governor is a rival of the First Minister and will take his place when the minister is arrested tomorrow. We will all go to my father's estates to see this scoundrel ousted."

The women cheered, but I saw some yawning. It was late and tomorrow would come soon.

* * * * *

The gate guard recognized me and gaped in surprise. "Mistress, what are you doing here?"

"I've come to get my home back." I gestured to the knife in my belt and the armed men at my back. He let us pass with a grin and a wave.

I went through the front door. The steward had changed little of the building except add more cushions for his comfort. I signaled for the men to stay in the receiving area and opened the screen to my father's office.

The steward sat at the low desk, busy scribbling in a ledger as he added coins to a heavy bag sitting at his side. He waved at me without looking up. "I told you not to bother me this morning."

"The last thing you told me was to leave my home."

He looked up in surprise.

"I'm here to take it back." I laid my hand on my knife.

"The samurai's daughter. I thought you long dead by now." His lips smiled, but his eyes shifted back and forth, looking for a way out. "Do you need a job? I have an opening for a laundress. Heavy loads and hot steam will take the stiffness out of your neck."

I took a step forward. He pushed back from the desk, scrambling to his feet. He topped me by a head and weighed three times more than I did.

"Afraid of a little girl?" I laughed.

His face went red and he clenched his fists. "Guards!" he shouted and waited. His face screwed into a scowl as he shouted again. "Guards."

"They're not coming." I reached into my tunic, grabbed a scroll, and waved it under his nose. "This is the order from the First Minister for your arrest."

"But the First Minister is my master! He wouldn't arrest me after all the money I've squeezed from this backwater province." He gestured toward the bag of coins.

"Your master is no longer the First Minister. He's been arrested for cursing the Regent and is on his way to the Oki Islands as we speak. You will join him there."

The color drained from the steward's face as he realized his fate. His body tensed and I readied my knife for an attack, but he grabbed the bag of money and rushed past me for the door.

I stuck out my foot and tripped him. He fell like a tree in the forest. The breath left his body in a whooshing sound. The coins spilled from the bag and rolled across the floor. The governor's men rushed into the room at the sounds, swords drawn, and pointed at the cowering man on the floor.

"Take him away." I sniffed and touched the man's fat thigh with my toe.

They pulled the steward to his feet and bound his hands behind him. As he started through the door, I thought of something. "Wait!"

He turned to me.

"My mother's jewelry? The gold dragon brooch?"

"I sold it long ago." He smirked at his minor triumph.

I shrugged, a pang in my heart for the loss. I didn't think he would still have it, but had to ask. They were my mother's, but they were only things–lovely things–but not important. I fingered the silk kerchief with the embroidered red bird tucked in my belt. The scent of jasmine always brought back memories of my mother and that was enough.

The guards shoved the steward roughly out the door. I followed to see the servants, the Ama, and the local farmers pelting him with rotten vegetables and slimy fish guts.

Namika saw me and approached. "Well, child, you've had your revenge."

I examined my feelings. Where was the sense of satisfaction at the greedy steward's downfall I had expected? I shook my head. "All I feel is pity. He could have chosen a different path and now his life is ruined."

"You are wise for one so young. I am glad your spirit has not been corrupted with thoughts of revenge." Namika patted my shoulder. "Now it is time to look to the future, not the past."

I turned back to the house I grew up in; the house I left over a year ago. It wouldn't feel right until I had scrubbed every last bit of the steward from the walls and aired out the rooms.

I smiled at Namika. I wouldn't have to do it alone. But it would need one more thing to feel like home.

Father.

19

AMA AND SAMURAI'S DAUGHTER

SHIMA TURNED OUT WITH FLAGS and fireworks when my father came home. The villainous First Minister took my father's place in banishment on the Oki Islands. No one shed tears as the guards trundled the greedy steward away in a wagon for prison. But, this day, I gave little thought to their fates or my role in bringing them to justice. My heart pounded and eyes strained as I watched for Father.

I stood at the head of the crowd flanked by local nobles, dressed as one of them in silk and jade. A sharp-eyed boy set up a cry, "They're coming! I see the banners!"

I wanted to jump up and down to see for myself, but I was no longer a wild Ama girl. I was again a noble samurai's daughter and must act the part.

The people greeted my father with cheers and hope.

The cheers started at the edge of town and rippled toward the center as Father rode in in a company of his own men. I spotted him sitting tall in the saddle, wearing light armor, but no helmet, the hilt of his sword stuck up over his shoulder. I searched his face as he drew nearer, looking for signs of his ordeal.

He looked thinner, but nothing scarred his handsome face. Of course, not all scars could be seen. I prayed to our ancestors that his kindness and good humor remained unbroken.

As he approached, he spotted me in the crowd. A smile lit up his face and he broke ranks, urging his horse into a fast trot. He arrived in front of me, dismounted in one smooth motion and gathered me into his arms.

I had dreamed of this moment for over a year. Now that it was real, I had trouble believing it.

"Tokoyo, my dearest girl," he whispered into my hair. "How I've longed to hold you, see you safe."

"Oh, Father!" My throat closed with tears, I couldn't say another word, only hold on to him as if my life depended on it.

The crowd murmured and milled at this public display of emotion. A single cheer erupted which spread through the throng until all were chanting, "Lord Oribe! Lord Oribe!"

Father turned to the crowd and motioned for silence. He put his arm around my shoulders. "Do not cheer for me, good people. I did nothing to obtain my release. All honor goes to my brave daughter Tokoyo! She traveled alone and friendless through the land and over the sea to free me. She found the cursed statue that proved my innocence. She fought and defeated the demon of the Oki Islands. Without her, the Regent would still be cursed, Yofune-Nushi would eat the children of Oki, and I would be in prison."

He turned to me, smiled and lifted me onto his horse. "Brave Tokoyo! The samurai's daughter!"

The crowd took up the chant and escorted us to a celebratory feast. I spotted Namika and Hana smiling at the edge of the crowd and waved. My heart swelled with love for my father and my friends.

It was true. I *was* a samurai's daughter.

But I could never have freed my father and the people of the Oki Islands without also being a humble Ama—a woman of the sea.

CULTURAL NOTES

Chapter 1

fundoshi – a long white loincloth that is tied around the lower body as an undergarment or swimwear. In some cases the cloth is very long to allow parts of it to hang forward almost as an apron

tenugui – a long thin kerchief that can be used as a washcloth or headband. They're often dyed in many colors and patterns. Tokoyo's headband is covered with phrases that bless the kerchief to protect and bring luck to the wearer

amagoya – a hut or small cottage in which a group of all female shellfish divers called the "Ama" live

Funadama – the goddess of the ocean in Shinto mythology. Fishermen and Ama divers pray to her for safe sailing and to catch lots of valuable fish/seafood.

Chapter 4

shiso – an herbal plant that is harvested and used to garnish or season food *kimono* – a traditional Japanese robe that consists of long graceful sleeves. It is worn on formal occasions and is made of silk with printed or embroidered designs.

obi – a long sash that is tied around the waist of one wearing a kimono. They can be tied in many decorative ways depending on the occasion and gender of the one wearing it.

Regent – a minister who manages and rules the state in place of the monarch, usually if they are too young or inexperienced. Regent Hojo Takatoki was appointed to rule as a representative of the Shogun Morikuni.

Chapter 9

kochosen – coin money that was used as currency from the Asuka to the Heian period in Japanese history. Copper coins were moderate in value while silver coins and gold coins were higher.

Kami – the spirits or energy that is found in everything in Shinto mythology. Kami can reside or manifest as anything from forces of nature, to animals, to even the souls of dearly departed. They can cause great good or great tragedy but all forms of Kami still have to be respected.

Chapter 15

Nami Amida Butsu – a Buddhist prayer to trust one's soul to celestial Buddha Amida for salvation and rebirth.

Yofune-Nushi – an evil water dragon in Japanese mythology who plagued a village with bad crops and shipwrecks. Villagers sacrificed a young maiden each year to make the dragon leave the village alone.

Blank Page Illustration

Tokoyo's name written in Japanese hiragana script.

AUTHOR'S NOTE

This story was inspired by a Japanese folktale called "The Tale of the Oki Islands" which I found in *Best-loved Folktales of the World* collected by Joanna Cole—one of my favorite children's authors. The story struck me as one of only two or three in the entire collection to feature a girl in an adventurous role. There were many women and girls who were rescued, many who were smart or tricky, but no other picked up a knife and fought a monster to rescue someone else. I read this story over thirty years ago and it haunted me.

Finally, I was in a place in my life where I could bring Tokoyo to a wider audience.

I dug up my tattered copy of *Best-loved Folktales* and traced the origins of the story to *Ancient Tales and Folk-lore of Japan* collected by Richard Gordon Smith and published in 1918. His entire collection is available free on the web along with thousands of other folktales at "The Internet Sacred Text Archive" (http://www.sacred-texts.com/shi/atfj/atfj19.htm). Smith explained that he sent "Oto, my Japanese hunter" to the remote Oki Islands and Oto brought back this story among others. I was amused to see that Smith styled

Tokoyo's father Oribe Shima as "the hero of this story" even though he does nothing but wait to be rescued by his daughter.

Smith also gives the approximate time and political situation at the time this tale was supposed to have happened and mentioned that Tokoyo had trained with the sea-diving women of her province. This gave me the idea to make this story as close to historical fiction as I could and minimize the fantasy elements. In my mind, Tokoyo became an ordinary girl who did extraordinary things based on her training and her personality—possibly helped by a magical knife—or her belief in a magical knife. You, Dear Reader, may choose your interpretation. My purpose is to entertain and inspire, not to dictate belief.

I was particularly taken with the Ama—"women of the sea"—the pearl divers of Japan and wanted to include more about them in Tokoyo's story. I think they were just as important as her father's training in preparing Tokoyo for her adventure. They were first mentioned in AD 750 in a collection of poems.

Women still work as Ama today, although in much fewer numbers because young women have more opportunities to work in much less dangerous jobs. Many Ama continue to work well into old age—some into their nineties. They work cooperatively and impose commonsense rules for fishery management on themselves. Japan has recommended that the Ama be recognized as a UNESCO Intangible Cultural Heritage.

My final hurdle in bringing this story to life was to decide how much of the complicated politics to put in the story. At the time, there was a hereditary Emperor with little power, a hereditary Shogun who normally had immense power, but was a minor and so he had a Regent that ruled for him. All the rulers had complicated webs of relatives and retainers who shuffled in and out of power, fought wars, etc. It was a chaotic time and I decided to include very little. This was Tokoyo's story, not her father's, so I only included the bits that help us understand what dangers Tokoyo meets.

I hope you enjoyed this story of Tokoyo as much as I enjoyed writing it. If you find other folktales about adventurous girls, please feel free to tell me about them at my website (faithljustice. com).

Thanks for reading!

ABOUT THE AUTHOR

FAITH L. JUSTICE writes award-winning fiction and articles in Brooklyn, New York. This is her first book for young people. For fun, she likes to dig in the dirt—her garden and various archaeological sites. Sample her work, check out her blog or ask Faith a question at her website:

faithljustice.com

ABOUT THE ILLUSTRATOR

KAYLA GILLIAM is an independent cartoonist living in the dense suburban forests of North Carolina. When she's not juggling her five dogs (Oreo, Domino, Max, Chewy and Baby) she enjoys researching Japanese culture.

Raggedy Moon Books